For my wife, Kathrin

Copyright © 1992 by Nord-Süd Verlag AG, Gossau Zürich, Switzerland
First published in Switzerland under the title *Hoppel findet einen Freund*
English translation copyright © 1992 by Rosemary Lanning

First published in the United States, Great Britain, Canada,
Australia and New Zealand in 1992 by North-South Books,
an imprint of Nord-Süd Verlag AG, Gossau Zürich, Switzerland.
First paperback edition published in 1995.

Distributed in the United States by North-South Books Inc., New York

Library of Congress Cataloging-in-Publication Data
Pfister, Marcus.
[Hoppel findet einen Freund. English]
Hopper hunts for spring / written and illustrated by Marcus
Pfister; translated by Rosemary Lanning.
Translation of: Hoppel findet einen Freund.
Summary: In looking for spring, Hopper meets some new animal friends.
[1. Animals—Fiction.   2. Spring—Fiction.]
PZ7.P448558Hq   1992
[E]—dc20   91-29671

British Library Cataloguing in Publication Data
Pfister, Marcus
Hopper hunts for spring.
I. Title   II. [Hoppel findet einen Freund. *English*]
833.914 [J]

ISBN 1-55858-139-1 (trade binding)
5 7 9 TB 10 8 6
ISBN 1-55858-147-2 (library binding)
3 5 7 9 LB 10 8 6 4
ISBN 1-55858-416-1 (paperback)
5 7 9 PB 10 8 6 4
Printed in Belgium

Hopper
Hunts for Spring

By Marcus Pfister

TRANSLATED BY

Rosemary Lanning

North-South Books
New York / London

"Wake up, Hopper," said his Mama. "The snow is beginning to melt. Spring is coming at last."

"Oh, great!" said Hopper excitedly. "Someone new to play with. I'll go and meet him."

Before his mother could explain that Spring isn't a person, Hopper was bounding away across the thin carpet of snow.

The snow had started to melt and blades of grass were pushing through it, reaching for the sun. In one place, where the snow had completely melted, Hopper found a hole next to a heap of earth.

"Hello! Is anyone at home?" he called.

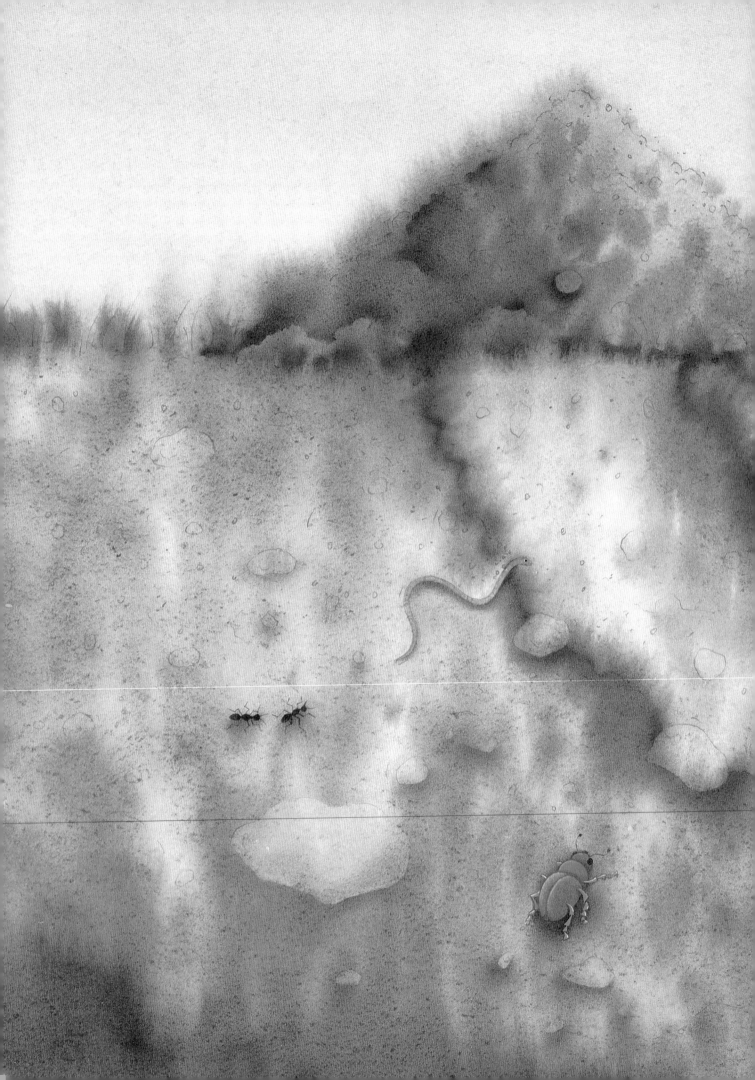

"Maybe *this* is where Spring lives," thought Hopper, squeezing himself into the hole. Inside, a dark tunnel sloped down into the earth. Hopper crept slowly down the tunnel. He couldn't see anything in the dark. Then he bumped into something soft.

"Hello," said Hopper. "You must be Spring. What are you doing in this tunnel?"

"Spring? Me?" said a voice. "No, I'm a mole and this is my tunnel. What are *you* doing here?"

"I'm looking for Spring."

"I don't know where Spring lives," said the mole as they
crawled out into the open air, "but his home must be larger
than this. Try the big cave on the other side of the forest...."

"Good-bye, mole, and thank you," said Hopper, scamper-
ing eagerly away.

Hopper soon found the cave. He peeped nervously inside.
Near the back was something big and brown. What could
it be?

"Wake up, Spring! It's me, Hopper. Mama and I are waiting
for you."

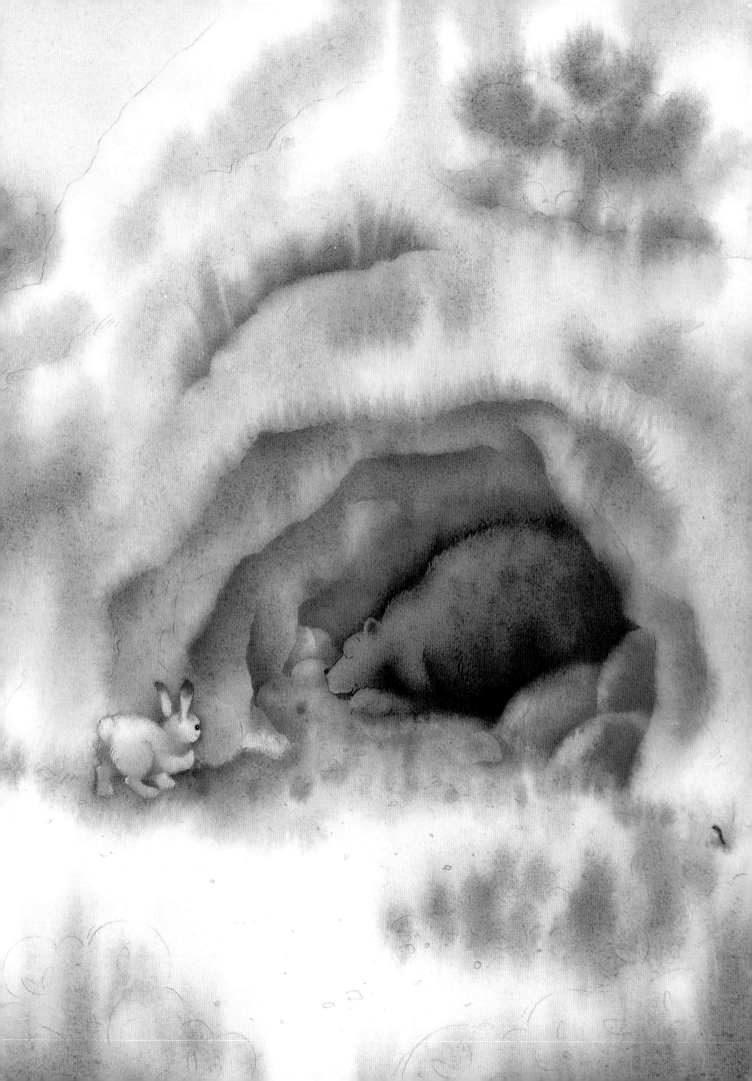

"Why must I wake up?" growled a deep voice. "Is winter over? Anyway, I'm not Spring, my little friend."

"Why not?"

"Well . . . because I'm a bear."

"Why are you sleeping in this cave?" asked Hopper.

"I always sleep here in winter. When the first snow falls, I crawl inside and don't wake up until Spring comes."

Hopper thought for a minute. Then he said, "My Mama says Spring is coming today. Do you know where he lives? I want to go and meet him."

The bear ambled up to the mouth of the cave and sniffed the air.

"You're right. It does smell of Spring. And if I'm not mistaken, the smell is coming from up there, in that tree. Perhaps that's where Spring lives."

They ran over to the tree.

"Wait here," said the bear. "I'll take a look." The bear clambered nimbly into the branches. Then he put one paw into a hole in the trunk.

"Honey!" he said, smacking his lips. "The perfect breakfast. I'm hungry after that long sleep. Spring doesn't seem to live here, though."

The bear climbed down again. Meanwhile, Hopper
had started to feel hungry too. They sat down together and
licked the delicious honey from the bear's paw.

"I'm not going to look for Spring anymore," sighed
Hopper. "I'm too tired. We'll just have to wait until
he comes."

"Let me take you home," said the bear kindly. "I need to stretch my legs. They are stiff from a whole winter's sleep. Come on, little one, climb onto my back and make yourself comfortable."

Night was falling when they found Mama hare.

"There you are, Hopper," she said. "I was getting worried."

"I didn't find Spring, Mama. He wasn't in the hole in the ground, or the bear's cave, or the hollow tree. I don't know where he's hiding."

"But Hopper, you can't go out and meet Spring," his Mama said softly. "Spring isn't an animal. It's just the time of year when the air gets warmer, the snow melts and the flowers start to bloom."

"Oh," said Hopper, disappointed.

"Don't be sad. You did find a new friend," said his mother.

Hopper crept close to Mama and waved good-bye to the bear. "Come back soon," he called after him. "We can play together all through the Spring."